A Break-of-Day Book

Ever since 1928, when Wanda Gág's classic *Millions of Cats* appeared, Coward-McCann has been publishing books of high quality for young readers. Among them are the easy-to-read stories known as Break-of-Day books. This series appears under the colophon shown above — a rooster crowing in the sunrise — which is adapted from one of Wanda Gág's illustrations for *Tales from Grimm*.

Though the language used in Break-of-Day books is deliberately kept as clear and as simple as possible, the stories are not written in a controlled vocabulary. And while chosen to be within the grasp of readers in the primary grades, their content is far-ranging and varied enough to captivate children who have just begun crossing the momentous threshold into the world of books.

COMMANDER TOAD in SPACE

by JANE YOLEN

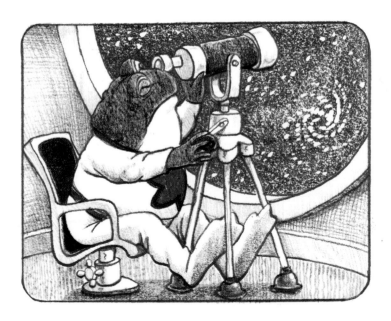

pictures by BRUCE DEGEN

The Putnam & Grosset Group

Text copyright © 1980 by Jane Yolen
Illustrations copyright © 1980, 1996 by Bruce Degen
All rights reserved. This book, or parts thereof, may not be
reproduced in any form without permission in writing from
the publisher. A PaperStar Book, published in 1996 by
The Putnam & Grosset Group, 200 Madison Avenue,
New York, NY 10016. PaperStar is a registered trademark
of The Putnam Berkley Group, Inc. The PaperStar logo is
a trademark of The Putnam Berkley Group, Inc.
Originally published in 1980 by Coward-McCann, Inc., New York.
Published simultaneously in Canada.
Printed in Hong Kong

Library of Congress Cataloging-in-Publication Data
Yolen, Jane H. Commander Toad in space.
Summary: The intrepid crew of the space ship "Star Warts"
lands on a water-covered planet inhabited by The Deep Wader,
a horrible hungry monster. [1. Toads—Fiction. 2. Monsters—
Fiction. 3. Science fiction.] I. Degen, Bruce. II. Title.
PZ7.Y78Co   [E]   ISBN 0-698-11355-1

10   9   8

For my spacey friends,
the MacLachlans:
Patty and Bob
John, Jamie and Emily
—JY

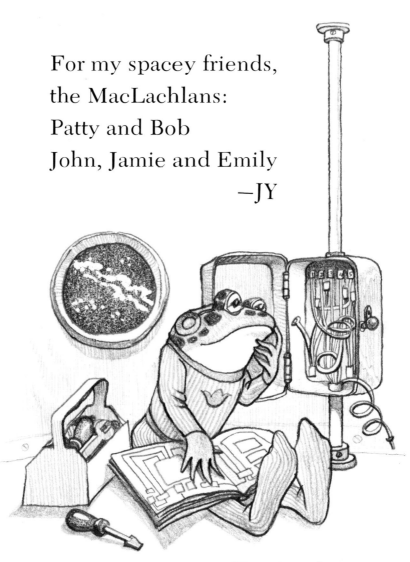

For Sarah
who loves frogs
—BD

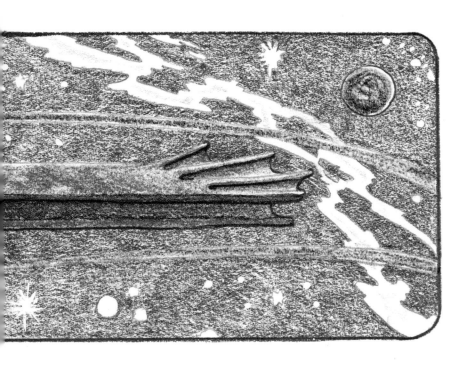

Long ships fly
between the stars.
Outside each porthole
worlds wink off and on.
There is one ship,
one mighty ship,
long and green,
that goes across the skies.

The captain of this ship
is brave and bright,
bright and brave.
There is no one
quite like him
in all the fleet.
His name is
COMMANDER TOAD.
His ship is the *Star Warts*.
Its mission: to go
where no spaceship
has gone before.
To find planets.
To explore galaxies.
To bring a little bit
of Earth
out to the alien stars.

Commander Toad
has a very fine crew.
The copilot is
Mr. Hop,
who thinks deep thoughts
behind his green face.
Lieutenant Lily
fixes engines.
She loves the big machines.

And young Jake Skyjumper
reads the maps
and plots the way
from star to star.
But the leader of them all
is COMMANDER TOAD,
brave and bright,
bright and brave.

11

What is it
that now shines
on the screen
with a strange
and shimmering light?
A brand-new world.
Commander Toad speaks:
"We will land
and look around
this brand-new world.

Jake Skyjumper,
you will stay on board.
You others,
come with me."
They get into
their special suits
and buckle on
their special guns.
"Just in case,"
says Commander Toad.
Lieutenant Lily smiles.
She is the best shot
in the whole crew.

They step aboard
the little sky skimmer
that will take them
from the mother ship
down to the planet below.
"Wait!"
It is young Jake
jumping toward them.
"I have just checked
this planet
with our computer.
The computer tells me
the planet is
made up of water.
There is nowhere to land."

Mr. Hop
shakes his head,
puts his hand
against his cheek,
closes his eyes
and begins to think.
Lieutenant Lily
stops smiling.
But Commander Toad
knows what to do.

He runs to
the ship's storeroom
and takes out something
big and soft and green
and puts it on the floor.
"What is *that*?"
asks Jake Skyjumper.
"A rubber lily pad,"
says Commander Toad.

Lieutenant Lily smiles.
"Just the thing," she says.
Mr. Hop opens his eyes.
They load the lily pad
and a hand pump
into the skimmer.
And last of all comes
COMMANDER TOAD.

The sky skimmer
leaves the mother ship.
It floats down
light as milkweed fluff,
noiseless as
a feather in the wind.
It hovers over
the watery world.

19

"Lieutenant," calls out
Commander Toad,
"drop our landing pad.
You'll be a
Lily with a lily.
Ha ha!"
He laughs at his own joke.

Lieutenant Lily opens the door.
She shoves out the pad.
It drifts down,
lazily down,
silently down,
and with a little *plop*
settles on the water.

Mr. Hop lets down a rope.
Then Lieutenant Lily,
the lightest of them all,
goes down the rope.
The pump is strapped
to her back.
She reaches the end,
flips over,
and holds the rope
between her legs.
She takes the pump
from her back
and starts to fill up
the lily pad.
Pump and pump and pump,
and the lily pad
is plump as a pillow.

Lieutenant Lily
jumps onto it
and bounces up and down
to test the pad.
It bobs in the water
and makes little waves.
But it does not sink.
Commander Toad
sets the sky skimmer down
until it fits
right into
the air-filled pad.

Out comes Mr. Hop.
He looks around.
And last of all comes
COMMANDER TOAD,
brave and bright,
bright and brave.

Mr. Hop
closes his eyes
and thinks cool thoughts
behind his green face.
Lieutenant Lily,
taking a rest,
puts her feet
over the side of the pad.
But Commander Toad
has no time
for such fiddle-faddle
and folderol.
He puts a hand
to his ear
and listens.

Then Mr. Hop
and Lieutenant Lily
listen, too.

They hear a sound,
low and angry,
coming up at them
from far below the waves.
At first it sounds
just like a hum.
Then it sounds
just like a buzz.
Then it sounds
just like a roar,
a roar with teeth.
"I AM DEEP WADER,"
says the roar.
"AND THIS PLANET
BELONGS TO ME!"

Bubbles burst
as loud as gunshots
by the side of the pad.
The roar gets closer.
The roar gets louder.
The roar breaks up and out
of the trembling waves.

Deep Wader
leaps high into the air.
He is black
and he is white.
He is dark
and he is light.
He is all colors.
He is no colors at all.
And he is very, very angry.

He snaps his many teeth.
He roars his awful roar.
Then he flips over
in the air
and disappears
beneath the shivering waves.

And now it is silent.
Too silent.
The silence is fear.
Into the silent fear
that Deep Wader left behind,
Mr. Hop speaks.
"I do not think
he will be gone for long,"
says Mr. Hop.

The other two
pay attention,
for Mr. Hop
is seldom wrong
when he has thought
long and hard
about something.
They listen
and through the silence
again they hear
the low and angry
hum—buzz—roar
coming up toward them.
Lieutenant Lily kneels
and aims her gun
at the place
where the roar will appear.

First the bubbles,
then the roar
break through the waves.
Then the monster
breaks through the waves.

Deep Wader
leaps up
and booms through his teeth:
"Mine. MINE. *MINE*!"
Lieutenant Lily shoots.

She hits Deep Wader
on his black skin,
on his white skin,
on his no-color-at-all skin.
But Deep Wader only laughs
as if the rays
tickle him.
And his laughter
is more horrible
than his roar.

He lands with a splash
and makes huge waves.
The lily pad is tossed
into the air
and almost tips over.
Lieutenant Lily
and Mr. Hop
and Commander Toad
all hold on.

But the sky skimmer
slips off the pad
and falls into the water.
Slowly it sinks
beneath the waves.

"Oh, no!" cries Lieutenant Lily.
"Now how will we ever leave?"
Mr. Hop
tries to think.
He closes his eyes.

Deep Wader swims lazily
on his back
toward the pad,
which is bobbing
like a ripe apple
in a pond.

40

He snaps his teeth
and each snap
makes another wave.
"My gun does not work
on this monster,"
says Lieutenant Lily.
"What should we do?
Think, Hop, think!"
But Mr. Hop
is all thought out,
and now the waves
are making him seasick.

Deep Wader gets closer.
His roar gets closer.
His teeth get closer.
His breath gets closer, too.
The lily pad rocks and rolls.
Commander Toad,
brave and bright,
bright and brave,
stands up at last.

He spreads his legs far apart
to keep himself from falling.
He takes a match
from his pocket.
"This might do the trick,"
says Commander Toad.

Mr. Hop opens his eyes.
He sighs.
"Oh, Commander,"
says Lieutenant Lily,
"if my gun
and Hop's head
do not work,
how can something
as small as a match help?"
"You keep Deep Wader busy,"
Commander Toad says,
"and leave the rest to me."

He takes out a small candle
and lights it with the match.
"I always carry candles,"
says Commander Toad,
"in case of birthdays
and other emergencies."
He pulls the plug
on the lily pad.
Air whooshes out,
then slows to
a gentle breeze.

Commander Toad
holds the candle
up to the air hole.
The flame flutters
but does not go out.
"Special candles,"
says Commander Toad.
"You can blow and blow
and blow some more
but they never go out."
Soon hot air begins to
fill up the lily pad.

Mr. Hop understands,
even before Lieutenant Lily.
"I will keep Deep Wader busy,"
says Mr. Hop.
"I have never yet met
a monster
who does not like riddles."
He turns and waves his hands.
He catches Deep Wader's eye.
"Mr. Wader," he calls,
"I have a monster riddle
just for you."

Deep Wader has never had
his very own riddle before.
He has never had anyone
to ask them.
He closes his mouth
and listens.

"What is a monster's
favorite ballet?"
asks Mr. Hop.
Deep Wader
opens his mouth again.
"*SWAMP LAKE!*" he roars.
He swims closer.
He no longer likes riddles.
"Keep him busy," calls
Commander Toad.
He lights another candle
and more hot air
goes into the pad.

Lieutenant Lily
was once on the stage
in a musical play
called *Warts and Peace.*
She starts to sing.
Deep Wader
starts to sing with her.
His singing is much worse
than his roar.

Commander Toad
lights a third candle.
The rubber lily pad
gets bigger
and bigger
and bigger.
It is a hot-air balloon.
It begins to float
one inch,
then two inches,
then a foot above the waves.

"NO MORE RIDDLES,
NO MORE SONGS,"
roars Deep Wader,
"LUNCH, HERE I COME."
"And here we go!"
calls out Commander Toad.
He puts his feet over the side
and paddles quickly in the air.
Lieutenant Lily
and Mr. Hop
do just the same.

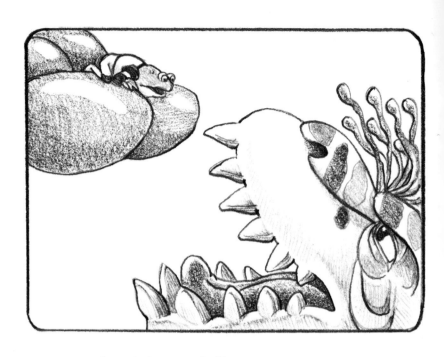

The lily pad floats
faster and faster
up into the air.
Deep Wader
watches his lunch
float away.
He leaps up
and snaps his teeth,
but he is too late.

Commander Toad
looks over the side
of the lily pad.
"We came in peace,"
he calls into Deep Wader's mouth.
"I'd like you better
in pieces," Deep Wader says.
"Nice *chewy* pieces."
He snaps his teeth again,
but the pad is out of reach.

"Just keep paddling,"
call Lieutenant Lily
and Mr. Hop.
Kick and kick
and kick some more,
and the lily pad rises.
The three space explorers
look at one another.
"That was close,"
says Mr. Hop.
Commander Toad agrees.
"But what about being brave?"
asks Lieutenant Lily.
"Bright and brave.
All we did was run away."

"You cannot be brave
in someone's stomach,"
says Mr. Hop.
"You cannot be brave
unless you are first
very much afraid,"
says Commander Toad.
"Well, I was certainly afraid,"
says Lieutenant Lily.
"And very, very brave,"
says Commander Toad.

"Keep kicking,"
says Mr. Hop.
And they kick the lily pad
all the way up
to the mother ship.
Young Jake Skyjumper
helps them aboard.

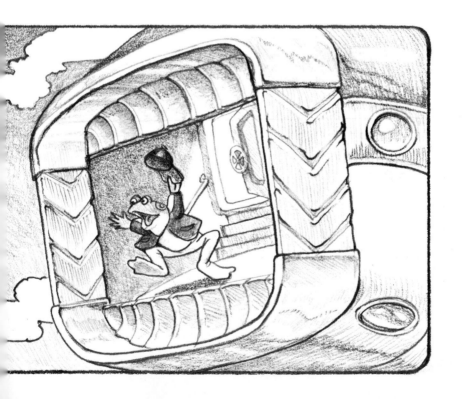

Then the ship takes off.
Brave and bright,
bright and brave,
Commander Toad
and his crew
swing *Star Warts*
into deep hopper space.
"Let's find some
new planets,"
says Commander Toad.
"Where we won't
have to be so brave,"
says Mr. Hop.
They all laugh.

Then they leapfrog
across the galaxy
from star
to star
to star.